Dear Parents and Educators,

Welcome to Penguin Young Readers! As parents and educators, you know that each child develops at his or her own pace—in terms of speech, critical thinking, and, of course, reading. Penguin Young Readers recognizes this fact. As a result, each Penguin Young Readers book is assigned a traditional easy-to-read level (1–4) as well as a Guided Reading Level (A–P). Both of these systems will help you choose the right book for your child. Please refer to the back of each book for specific leveling information. Penguin Young Readers features esteemed authors and illustrators, stories about favorite characters, fascinating nonfiction, and more!

Me and My Robot

LEVEL 2

GUIDED READING LEVEL **G**

This book is perfect for a **Progressing Reader** who:
- can figure out unknown words by using picture and context clues;
- can recognize beginning, middle, and ending sounds;
- can make and confirm predictions about what will happen in the text; and
- can distinguish between fiction and nonfiction.

Here are some **activities** you can do during and after reading this book:
- In this story, Lucy loses her kitten. It is a mystery as to where her kitten has gone! Reese gives Robot clues to help solve the mystery of the missing kitten. For example, he says, "A kitten is small." Pretend Lucy loses something else, such as a book or a soccer ball. Come up with a list of clues that you could give Robot to help find the missing items.
- Sight Words: Sight words are frequently used words that readers must know just by looking at them. These words are known instantly, on sight. Knowing these words helps children develop into efficient readers. As you read the story, point out the sight words below.

have	his	play	some	where
help	know	said	what	your

Remember, sharing the love of reading with a child is the best gift you can give!

—Bonnie Bader, EdM
  Penguin Young Readers program

*Penguin Young Readers are leveled by independent reviewers applying the standards developed by Irene Fountas and Gay Su Pinnell in *Matching Books to Readers: Using Leveled Books in Guided Reading*, Heinemann, 1999.

For Terry—CR

Penguin Young Readers
Published by the Penguin Group
Penguin Group (USA) Inc., 375 Hudson Street, New York, New York 10014, USA
Penguin Group (Canada), 90 Eglinton Avenue East, Suite 700, Toronto, Ontario M4P 2Y3, Canada
(a division of Pearson Penguin Canada Inc.)
Penguin Books Ltd., 80 Strand, London WC2R 0RL, England
Penguin Group Ireland, 25 St. Stephen's Green, Dublin 2, Ireland (a division of Penguin Books Ltd.)
Penguin Group (Australia), 250 Camberwell Road, Camberwell, Victoria 3124, Australia
(a division of Pearson Australia Group Pty. Ltd.)
Penguin Books India Pvt. Ltd., 11 Community Centre, Panchsheel Park, New Delhi—110 017, India
Penguin Group (NZ), 67 Apollo Drive, Rosedale, Auckland 0632, New Zealand
(a division of Pearson New Zealand Ltd.)
Penguin Books (South Africa) (Pty.) Ltd., 24 Sturdee Avenue,
Rosebank, Johannesburg 2196, South Africa

Penguin Books Ltd., Registered Offices: 80 Strand, London WC2R 0RL, England

Text copyright © 2003 by Tracey West. Illustrations copyright © 2003 by Cindy Revell. All rights reserved.
First published in 2003 by Grosset & Dunlap, an imprint of Penguin Group (USA) Inc. Published in 2012
by Penguin Young Readers, an imprint of Penguin Group (USA) Inc., 345 Hudson Street, New York,
New York 10014. Manufactured in China.

Library of Congress Control Number: 2002151238

ISBN 978-0-448-42895-6   10 9 8 7 6 5 4 3 2 1

Me and My Robot

by Tracey West
illustrated by Cindy Revell

Penguin Young Readers
An Imprint of Penguin Group (USA) Inc.

This is me.

My name is Reese.

This is my robot.

His name is Robot.

Robot and I have

fun together.

We play games.

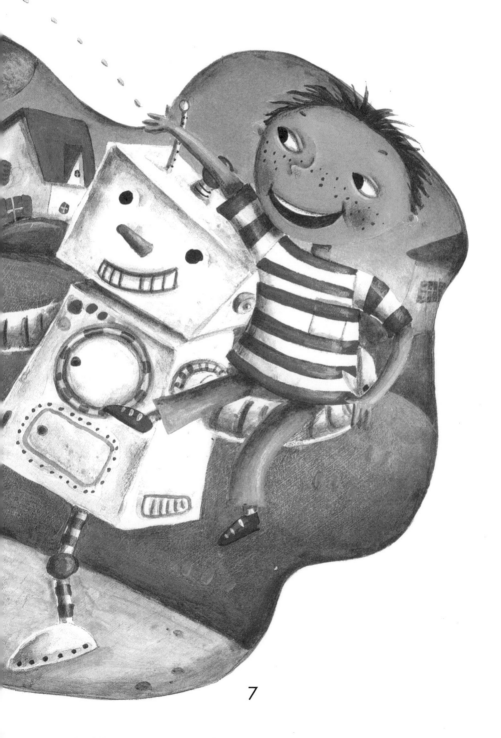

We go for rides.

We play with my friends.

One day Lucy came to see

Robot and me.

"WHAT IS A KITTEN?"

Robot asked.

"I need help," Luc

"I have lost my new

"Robot and I will h

"We will find your k

Robot led us to a big dog.

"This is not my kitten!" Lucy said.

"A kitten is small," I told Robot.

"FOLLOW ME!" Robot said.

Robot led us to some ants.

"These are not my kitten!" Lucy said.

"A kitten is soft and furry,"

I told Robot.

"FOLLOW ME," Robot said.

21

Robot led us to a squirrel.

"That is not my kitten!" Lucy said.

"A kitten lives in a house,

not a tree," I told Robot.

"FOLLOW ME," Robot said.

Robot led us to a rabbit.

"That is not my kitten," Lucy said.

Then Lucy showed us a picture.

"This is my kitten," she said.

"I SEE!" said Robot.

"YOUR KITTEN IS SMALL.

IT IS SOFT.

IT IS FURRY.

IT LIVES IN A HOUSE.

I KNOW WHERE YOUR

KITTEN IS."

"Where?" I asked.

"Where is Lucy's kitten?"

"RIGHT HERE," said Robot.

"I LIKE KITTENS!" said Robot.